LAMAN LIBRARY

3 7910 50204338 0

DISCARDED

D1088771

Charles M. Schulz

Travels with My Cactus

HarperHorizon

An Imprint of HarperCollinsPublishers

William F. Laman Public Library
2801 Orange Street
North Little Rock, Arkansas 72114

First published in 1998 by HarperCollins*Publishers* Inc. http://www.harpercollins.com. Copyright © 1998 United Feature Syndicate, Inc. All rights reserved. HarperCollins ® and ♨ ® are trademarks of HarperCollins*Publishers* Inc. *Travels with My Cactus* was published by HarperHorizon, an imprint of HarperCollins*Publishers* Inc., 10 East 53rd Street, New York, NY 10022. Horizon is a registered trademark used under license from Forbes Inc. PEANUTS is a registered trademark of United Feature Syndicate, Inc. PEANUTS © United Feature Syndicate, Inc. Based on the PEANUTS ® comic strip by Charles M. Schulz. http://www.unitedmedia.com. ISBN 0-694-01048-0. Printed in China.

"Each Halloween I sit in this pumpkin patch waiting for the Great Pumpkin to appear. This year I know he's going to come!"

"What was that? I heard a noise!
Is it? It *is*!"

"The Great Pumpkin!"

"I saw him, Charlie Brown! I saw him! Last night I saw the Great Pumpkin!"

"Linus, there's a cactus standing over there in the pumpkin patch . . . You must have seen it. You were there on Halloween night."

"It was kind of dark."

William F. Laman Public Library
2801 Orange Street
North Little Rock, Arkansas 72114